26 TIPS ★ FOR SURVIVING GRADE 6

BY: CATHERINE AUSTEN

JAMES LORIMER & COMPANY LTD.,

PUBLISHERS

James Lorimer & Company Ltd., Publishers acknowledges the support
of the Ontario Arts Council. We acknowledge the financial support
of the Government of Canada through the Canada Book Fund for
our publishing activities. We acknowledge the support of the Canada
Council for the Arts which last year invested $20.1 million in writing
and publishing throughout Canada. We acknowledge the Government
of Ontario through the Ontario Media Development Corporation's
Ontario Book Initiative.

Cover Design: Meghan Collins
Cover Image: iStockphoto

Library and Archives Canada Cataloguing in Publication

Austen, Catherine,
      26 tips for surviving grade 6 / Catherine Austen.

Issued also in an electronic format.
ISBN 978-1-55277-925-5 (bound).--ISBN 978-1-55277-924-8 (pbk.)

      I. Title. II. Title: Twenty-six tips for surviving grade six.

PS8601.U785T84 2011   jC813'.6   C2011-903907-9

James Lorimer &
Company Ltd., Publishers
317 Adelaide Street West,
Suite 1002
Toronto, ON, Canada
M5V 1P9
www.lorimer.ca

Distributed in the
United States by:
Orca Book Publishers
P.O. Box 468
Custer, WA USA
98240-0468

Printed and bound in Canada.
Manufactured by Friesens in Altona, Manitoba, Canada in August, 2011.
Job # 67776

To my sixth grade BFF, Stefanie Black, and to Mike Gray, for the circus.

– C.A.

Lesson 1: Social Studies

Tips for Making a New Friend

#1: People do not always need your help.

Becky Lennox lived by the river in a little house with a big yard. She had a dog that didn't drool and a teenage brother who did. She had a red bicycle and a pink bedroom. She had good grades and great ideas. She had everything she wanted — until Violet Turnbull moved to town.

The trouble began on the first day of fall. Becky stepped outside and felt a change in the air. The sun shone. The birds sang. But summer was over.

Becky walked to the curb to wait for the school bus. Her mother followed her, carrying a hand spade and a bag of tulip bulbs. It looked like gardening, but Becky knew it was spying. "Can you go back in the house?" she asked.

"No," her mother said. "I tried planting bulbs in the house once. It didn't work."

"You're embarrassing me," Becky added.

"I'll hide behind a tree when the bus comes," her mom said. "No one will know I was ever here."

"The new girl knows you're here," Becky said. She pointed down the street, where Violet Turnbull stood in front of a large brick house.

Violet was tall and slim, with blond hair cut below her chin. She wore white jeans with a red T-shirt and black sneakers. She held a pile of pebbles in her left hand and threw them, one by one, at the SOLD sign in her yard.

Becky's mother waved and screamed, "Hello there! You must be Violet!"

"Unbelievable," Becky muttered.

Her brother, Jason, walked outside, wearing pyjama bottoms and eating dry Cheerios straight from the box. "What's up?" he asked. "Is your bus late? Hey, is that the new girl?" He raised an arm and waved at Violet, exposing all his naked armpit hair.

Violet waved back.

Becky tried to disappear behind the hedge. Her mother put an arm around her shoulder. "She seems nice," she said. "You should sit with her on the bus."

"Why not go wait with her?" Jason said. "She'll be nervous starting school three weeks late. Go welcome her to the neighbourhood."

"Please go in the house," Becky begged. "Both of you."

"Promise me you'll help her out?" her mom said.

"I promise," Becky said.

But Violet Turnbull did not need Becky's help. She was smart, she was cute, and she was fun. She started school on Friday morning, and by the time the lunch bell rang, she was the most popular girl in Becky's class.

"I don't mind if you sit with me," Becky said to her in the cafeteria.

"Thanks." Violet smiled and sat down. But there was ketchup on her chair, so she spent the lunch hour running home to change her pants.

In gym class, Becky whispered, "I'll go easy on you because you're new."

"Thanks," Violet said. Then she stole the

basketball from Becky's team twenty times in a row.

"I'll save you a seat on the bus," Becky offered after school.

"No, thanks," Violet replied. Then she hopped into her mother's red convertible.

Becky sat alone on the ride home. She wondered how the day had gone so wrong.

When the bus stopped at a red light, Becky saw Violet's car in the lane beside it. It looked expensive. Violet's mother tapped the steering wheel with long, red fingernails. She wore a black suit, black sunglasses, and red lipstick. She looked like she was late for an important meeting.

Violet looked up at the bus and waved. Becky began to wave back, but the girls in the seat ahead of her jumped up and opened their window. "Hey, Violet! Cool car!" they shouted. "Have a great weekend! See you Monday!"

Becky sighed and turned away. Across the street, she saw an advertisement for an expensive law firm. *Some people can sell their help for thousands of dollars,* she thought. *I can't even give mine away.*

Becky had one weekend to scoop Violet for a best friend before the rest of the class had a chance. On Saturday morning, she walked down her street six times. "Take the dog so you don't look so weird," her brother advised. Champ ran for his leash. Becky hoped they would run into Violet. But Violet's yard was always empty.

On Sunday morning, Becky took cookies to Violet's house. She hoped that Violet would ask her in. But no one answered the door.

On Sunday night, Becky ate nine cookies. She didn't feel any better.

On Monday morning, Becky sat on the school bus next to her friend Stacey.

Violet sat across from them. "Do you guys play after-school sports?" she asked.

"I play soccer twice a week," Becky said.

Stacey nodded. "Becky's a great goalie."

But in gym class that morning, Violet kicked ten soccer balls into Becky's net. "Sports camp three summers in a row," she said.

On Tuesday, Becky walked to school alone. She had a presentation to give in geography class, so she practised her speech in her head.

She told her class all about Arctic wildlife. She passed out pictures of polar bears and ptarmigans. She kept her cue cards in order. Her cheeks grew pink and her throat grew dry, but she finished without any mistakes.

"Good work, Becky," said her teacher, Miss Nancy. "It's your turn, Violet."

Violet talked about the Arctic, too. She didn't pass out pictures or use cue cards. Instead, she gave a hilarious slide show of her spring trip to the Yukon. She showed pictures of caribou fawns, northern lights, baby geese, and tiny trees. She told a funny story with every picture. The last photo showed Violet sharing an apple with an Arctic fox. The whole class applauded.

"Don't you get nervous?" Becky asked afterward.

Violet shook her head. "I took public speaking lessons last year."

Becky couldn't tell if that was a joke.

In Wednesday's art

class, Becky knocked two jars of paint off the table. "I'm sorry, Miss Nancy," she said. "I'll clean it up."

"Wait!" Violet shouted. She stirred the blue and yellow paint on the floor and turned Becky's mess into a lush green forest.

"Let's let it dry just like that!" Miss Nancy said.

"Unbelievable," Becky muttered.

"March break camp at the art gallery," Violet said with a wink.

On Thursday, Becky looked forward to music class. She played "Three Blind Mice" on the clarinet. Violet played "Ode to Joy" on the piano. Miss Nancy called in the principal. He clapped for a very long time.

"Music lessons?" Becky asked.

Violet smiled. "Twice a week since forever."

Becky was not enjoying school this year.

On Friday morning, Becky rode her Walmart skateboard to school.

"Wait for me!" Violet called. She zoomed up on her custom-made board.

Becky lost her balance and crashed into Violet. "Sorry," she said.

"No problem." Violet fixed her knee pads and smiled. "Everybody fails when they're just learning."

Becky sighed. She had been skateboarding for two years.

She could not wait for the day to end. She rode her skateboard home alone, not paying attention to where she was going.

A turtle crossed the sidewalk ahead of her. It was not as fast as a skateboard. "Watch out, slowpoke!" Becky shouted.

She stuck her tongue out at the turtle.

Then she noticed Violet behind her.

Violet hopped off her skateboard, gently picked up the turtle, and carried it to the grass where it would be safe.

Becky wanted to cry. *Isn't it enough that she's cool?* she thought. *Does she have to be kind, too?*

#3: Be yourself – unless you're mean and jealous and a total jerk, in which case, try to be someone else.

On Saturday, Becky played road hockey at Stacey's house. She was having fun until Violet joined in. Then her team quickly lost its lead. They would have lost the game, but Violet took pity on them and called it a tie.

Becky stomped home.

"I have good news, honey," her mother said. "I invited Violet over for dinner."

"I just got away from her," Becky whined. She whacked the floor with her hockey stick.

Her mother frowned. "Put that in the shed."

Outside, Champ dropped a toy rabbit at Becky's feet. Becky played tug until the rabbit split in half. That made her feel better.

Becky's mother carried a plate of chocolate chip oatmeal cookies onto the deck. "I thought you'd want to see Violet tonight," she said.

"I never want to see her again," Becky groaned.

Her mother frowned. "You waited years for someone your age to move to this street."

"Now I understand the saying, 'Be careful what you wish for.'"

Becky's mother offered a warm cookie. "Don't you like Violet?" she asked.

"I told you what she's like."

"You said she's perfect."

"Exactly!"

Her mother laughed. "She'll be here in an hour," she said. "You should wash up."

Becky peeled off her mud-stained jeans and washed her greasy hair. She tried to stay in the bathroom, faking a stomach sickness, but no one believed her.

"I need a shower!" Jason shouted when he got home from football practice. He banged on the bathroom door.

Becky plugged her nose and let him in.

"Very funny," Jason said. He stripped off his sweaty jersey and waved it in her face. She screamed and ran to the kitchen. She chomped another oatmeal cookie.

Outside, Becky's father was cutting the lawn with a push mower. His hair was speckled with grass clippings. His face was sweaty and pink. The toes of his sneakers were green.

"Your dad looks tired," her mother said.

Becky nodded. "Even his pants look tired," she said. "They're falling down." She didn't want Violet to see her dad like this. She thought Violet's father probably mowed his lawn in a suit and tie.

"Here comes Violet now," her mom said. "Wow! She has a motorized scooter."

"I'm going to be sick," Becky muttered. She brushed the cookie crumbs off her chest and accidentally smeared chocolate all over her white T-shirt.

The evening did not begin well. Everyone sat on the back deck drinking lemonade and munching vegetable sticks.

"What's the Yukon like, Violet?" Becky's mother asked.

"I heard that it's a fly-infested wasteland," Becky said.

Her father cleared his throat. "Have you visited the recreation centre up the street, Violet? There's a swimming pool and a skate park."

"Violet has a backyard pool," Becky said. "She can stay home."

Jason tossed a carrot at Becky's head. "Where did you get your scooter, Violet?" he asked.

"Jason asked for a motorized scooter for his grade eight graduation present," Becky told Violet. "But Mom and Dad said they're for lazy kids."

"Becky!" her mother shouted.

"But that's what you said," Becky argued.

Her family glared at her.

Violet stared at the table.

Becky slurped lemonade and tapped her feet.

"Becky, why don't you show Violet your room?" her dad suggested.

"I'd like a word with you first," her mom said.

"Don't bother," Becky said. "I already know." *Parents always tell you to express your feelings*, she thought, *but they only mean it when you have something good to say.*

#4: Put your best foot forward, even if your shoes are dorky.

"Your brother is really cute," Violet whispered upstairs.

Becky made a face. "Are you crazy?"

Violet shrugged. She turned to Becky's bookcase. "You like medieval history?" she asked.

Becky did not answer.

"I like medieval history," Violet said. "I have a collection of model knights my dad bought in France."

"I have something just as good," Becky said. She opened her closet and dragged out a castle as tall as her waist.

The walls were made of small grey stones. Inside them, tiny people fed chickens and hammered iron in a brown dirt courtyard. A wooden stable housed twelve tiny horses, and an armoury stored dozens of miniature weapons. In the very centre of the castle walls stood a tall stone keep. Becky swung open the roof to reveal a royal banquet hall filled with lords and ladies.

"Where did you get this?" Violet exclaimed. "I would love one of these!"

"You can't buy it," Becky informed her. "My mom made it for me."

"It's the coolest castle I've ever seen," Violet said.

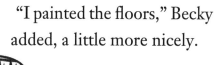

"I painted the floors," Becky added, a little more nicely.

"Your mother let you help?" Violet asked.

Becky shook her head. "She *made* me help."

"You are *so* lucky," Violet whispered. "Am I allowed to touch it?"

"Of course."

Violet picked up a model chicken. "There's even a tiny egg!" she shouted.

Becky smiled. "It's pretty impressive, isn't it?"

"It's beautiful," Violet said, replacing the chicken.

Becky shrugged. "I don't really play with it anymore." She picked up a deck of playing cards and began shuffling. "What's your favourite card game? Poker? Crazy eights? War?"

Violet shrugged. "I only know solitaire."

Becky crashed onto her bed. "Are you serious? Doesn't your family play cards? What do you do if it rains when you're camping?"

"My family never goes camping."

"What do you do all summer?" Becky asked. "Oh, wait. I know. You go to the Arctic and feed the foxes."

Violet closed the castle roof. "I only went there once," she said. "Usually I go to camp."

"Oh yeah," Becky said. "Music camp, sports camp, art camp, public-speaking camp, become-a-perfect-person camp."

Violet rolled her eyes. "I have to go *some-where* for the holidays."

"What do you do at Christmas?" Becky asked.

"We visit my mother's family."

"Where do they live?"

Violet stared at the castle and muttered something Becky couldn't hear.

"Where?" Becky repeated.

Violet looked up and said, "Italy."

Becky laughed. "How lucky can you be?"

Violet laughed, too. "I know. Sometimes

my grandparents take me to other parts of Europe. Last year, we went to Scotland. That was my favourite trip."

"So you've seen real castles?" Becky asked.

Violet nodded. "They're huge, with lots of secret passages."

"Wow," Becky said. "I bet you'd give a good slide show on castles."

Violet sat on the bed next to Becky. "I wouldn't want to live in a castle," she said. "They're dark and cold. The rooms are too big, and I kept getting lost in the hallways. They were a bit creepy. I'd rather live in a house like this."

"Our house is small," Becky said. "Yours is almost a mansion."

Violet shrugged. "My parents have offices at home so they can work in the evenings." She pointed to Becky's hands. "I like the way you shuffle two stacks of cards at the same time."

Becky had almost forgotten she was holding the cards. "Let's play Crazy Eights," she said. "I'll teach you. I'm an expert. I never lose."

Becky lost to Violet five hands out of six. She was happy to hear her mother call them for dinner.

"You're an awesome shuffler," Violet whispered as they walked downstairs.

At least I'm good at something, Becky thought.

#5: Sometimes what you need to change is your point of view.

After dinner, Becky taught Violet how to play poker. Then they asked Becky's brother to play.

Jason rolled his eyes like he was doing them a favour. He changed his attitude after Violet won all his poker chips.

"I can't believe you just learned this game tonight, Violet," Jason said. "It's like you've been playing cards for years."

"I don't play the cards," Violet said with a proud smile. "I play the man."

Becky laughed. "I taught her everything she knows."

"It's true," Violet said. "She did."

"Jason!" Becky's dad called from the kitchen. "Your friends are here!"

Two boys dressed in baggy jeans and T-shirts walked into the dining room. Jason gave them high-fives and introduced them to Violet. "These are my friends, Steve and Terry."

Becky's mom peeked out from the kitchen. "Can you boys drag my kids outside so I can wipe the table?"

"Sure, Mrs. Lennox," Steve said.

Terry pulled a video game from his jacket and raised his eyebrows.

"Later," Jason said. "First let's take the kids outside."

"We're not kids," Becky said. "We're preteens."

Jason laughed. "You're kids."

"You're kids, too," Violet told him.

"No. We're teenagers," Jason argued. "We're almost adults."

Becky's mom peeked out from the kitchen again. "You're all kids," she said. "Now go outside and get some fresh air until the sun sets, like kids are supposed to do."

Outside, the boys convinced the girls to play hide-and-seek commando freeze-tag, a game with extremely complicated rules that Jason had invented last summer.

"I don't get it," Violet whispered to Becky.

"Just go where I go," Becky said.

Terry and Steve ran into the backyard hollering while Jason counted backward from thirty.

Becky took Violet by the hand. "Come on! We have to hide."

"How about up the tree?" Violet asked. "These low branches make a great ladder."

Becky looked up to the top of the spruce tree. She shuddered. "I don't like heights."

"That's perfect," Violet said. "Your brother will never look for us up there." She stepped one foot onto the lowest branch.

"No!" Becky shouted. "I mean, I'm *terrified* of heights." She looked at her feet and said, "I have a bit of a phobia. Don't tell anyone."

Violet hopped onto the ground. "Oh, okay. I feel that way about rats."

In the front yard, Jason shouted, "Five! Four! —"

"Quick!" Becky exclaimed, grabbing Violet's arm. She ran straight to the doghouse and crawled inside. "I hope Champ didn't bring any dead rats in here," she muttered.

"You're really lucky," Violet said when they were safely hidden among Champ's toys. "My family never does fun stuff together. We don't even do boring stuff."

"We do a *lot* of boring stuff," Becky said. "Now hush. It looks like Terry is frozen and Steve joined Jason's army."

Violet shook her head. "I don't understand this game. But I like your family, Becky. Maybe you could adopt me."

Becky turned to her with a frown.

"Then we'd be sisters," Violet added.

"My parents don't want any more children," Becky said with a grin.

"Then we'll have to be best friends," Violet said. "I think you'd make a great best friend, Becky."

Becky looked at Violet's sweet, smart, and smiling face. She smiled back. Then she left Violet in the doghouse and raced to the front yard. "Last one to the oak tree is It!" she shouted.

Because sometimes you have to let a friend find you, Becky thought.

Lesson 2: Science

Tips for Understanding the Human Male

#6: Don't mess with male teachers.

Becky didn't hear a word her substitute teacher said during math class. She had more important things on her mind. Like the note Scott Sherman had just sent her.

It was written on a torn piece of binder paper that had been folded four times and addressed with the initials B.L., for Becky Lennox. It read, *Do you want to go to the circus on Saturday?* It was signed with the initials S.S., followed by the name *Scott* in brackets.

It had hit Becky in the back of the head five minutes ago. That didn't seem like a nice way to send a love note, but boys are sometimes confusing.

Scott Sherman was the cutest boy in the world, but only Becky seemed to think so. Most of the girls in her class thought Scott's friend Nick was cuter. Becky thought those girls were crazy.

Scott had drawn two boxes at the bottom of his note, with the words *YES* and *NO* beside them.

Becky didn't know which box to check. Of course she wanted to go to the circus with Scott. But Saturday was Halloween. She had plans to trick-or-treat with Violet. She tried to explain her problem by mouthing the word *Halloween* and making monster faces. That didn't work. The substitute teacher yelled at her, and Scott just thought she was being weird.

A second note hit her in the back of the head. *In the afternoon*, it read. Problem solved.

Becky checked the *YES* box on Scott's first note. She folded the paper four times. She waited until the teacher turned his back. Then she threw the note at Scott.

He read it and gave Becky a thumbs-up.

Becky kicked her heels together and blushed.

At the desk beside her, Violet faked a stretch. She stuck out her arms and dropped a slip of paper onto Becky's desk. *What's up?* it read.

Becky wrote back, *Scott asked me to the circus on Saturday*

afternoon!

Violet scribbled on the note for a long time before passing it back. *Great!* it read. *Nick asked me to the circus, too! He won four free tickets. Scott's mom said she would take the four of us. Isn't that awesome?*

That didn't feel entirely awesome to Becky. She scribbled a quick reply. *I LOVE SCOTT, BUT YOU DON'T EVEN LIKE NICK!*

Violet laughed. She wrote back, *But I like circuses.*

Becky huffed. She was trying to think of a clever response when a dark shadow clouded her desk and a huge hairy hand grabbed her note.

Becky looked up. The substitute teacher towered beside her. She had forgotten his name. She had forgotten he was even in the room. She watched him silently read the secrets of her heart. He made a noise like a snicker.

Becky trembled in fear. This total stranger held her life in his hands. He could make her read the note in front of the class. He could ruin her whole life in his one lousy day of substitute teaching!

The teacher walked to the front of the room. He said, "Miss Lennox, I would like you to read something to the class."

Becky held her head in her hands.

At the desk beside her, Violet whimpered. Scott groaned from the desk behind her.

The teacher stared at each of them in turn. Then he said, "Please read question three on page twenty-six of the textbook. Then explain the correct answer to the class."

Becky thought she'd misheard. "What?" she squeaked.

"Question three, page twenty-six!" the teacher barked.

Becky sat up and smiled. "Sure!"

She got the answer wrong and had to do extra homework, but she didn't care. She just said, "Thank you."

Teachers are strange and unpredictable, she thought. *Especially male teachers. And that's just a fact of life.*

#7: All dads are weird.

"Can I go to the circus with Scott?" Becky asked her parents.

"On Halloween afternoon?" her mom said. "You won't get home until five o'clock. That doesn't give you much time to get ready."

"It's plenty of time," Becky said.

Her mother sighed. "You said you would decorate the yard with me."

"We could do that next year," Becky said.

"All right," her mom said. "As long as

you're back in time for dinner, it's fine by me." She smiled and added, "You're growing up so fast."

"Too fast!" Becky's father said. "Just who is this boy?"

"Scott Sherman used to come over on play dates when they were in kindergarten," Becky's mom reminded him. "He's very nice and quiet."

Becky's dad frowned. "Can quiet boys really be trusted?" he asked. "What are his grades like?"

"What does that matter?" Becky asked.

Her dad crossed his arms and scowled. "Has he ever failed a grade? Just how old is this boy?"

"He's eleven. And no, he hasn't failed any grades. He's a B student," Becky said.

"So he's not an *A* student," her dad said, shaking his head.

"*I'm* an A student," Becky reminded him.

"Exactly," her mother said. "And you respect yourself and your feelings enough to demand that boys treat you with respect, too. Right?"

Becky shrugged. "I guess so."

"You *guess* so?" her dad repeated. "If you don't *know* so, then you're too young for boys. Does this Scott person really expect us to let you to go to the circus unsupervised?"

"His mom will be there!" Becky said.

"She's a total stranger," her dad argued.

"Actually, we've met her many times," Becky's mom said. "She's on the school's parent council."

Becky's dad grunted. "Maybe Jason could chaperone them."

"I don't go to circuses!" Jason shouted

from upstairs in his bedroom, where he was busy eavesdropping. "They're cruel! Animals should not be used for entertainment!"

"I don't need a chaperone," Becky told her parents. "I've gone out with friends a hundred times before."

"Not *boy*friends," her dad argued.

"Scott's not my boyfriend," Becky said.

"Of course not," her mother said. "You're much too young for a boyfriend."

"You're much too young for a circus," her father added.

Her mom laughed. "She's not *joining* the circus, dear. She'll be fine."

"How much does it cost?" her dad asked. "It better not be more than twenty dollars."

"It's free," Becky said.

Her father paced the room, huffing. Then he called Scott's parents to find out who would be driving and how old their car was and what

sort of emergency plan they had in case anyone was lost or left alone for a single second.

"Is it just you watching the two kids?" he
asked Mrs. Sherman over the phone. "I see.
That sounds fine. We'll see you Saturday at
noon." He hung up and turned to Becky with
a smile. "You didn't say Violet was going with
you."

"What difference does that make?" Becky
asked.

Her dad chuckled. "It's a whole
different situation with Violet
there — more like a group
of friends than a date. She's
such a responsible girl."

"So am I," Becky said.

Her dad nodded.
"Sure you are, sweetie.
And Mrs. Sherman
sounds awfully strict.

She'll keep you and Scott in line just fine." He patted Becky's shoulder and left the room with a smile.

Becky frowned. She was happy that she was allowed to go, but angry that her father trusted everyone in the world except her. "Why is Dad so weird?" she asked her mother.

Her mom just shrugged. "So tell me about Scott," she whispered.

Becky smiled. *Fathers are not like mothers*, she thought. *I am so lucky to have one of each.*

#8: Brothers always embarrass you.

"I can't believe you're going to a circus that has animal acts!" Jason shouted at Becky. "I showed you my pamphlets. Circuses are cruel. If you go to the circus, you're supporting cruelty." He pointed to Champ, who lay on the carpet with his front paws crossed. "Imagine somebody whipping and prodding him through a hoop."

Champ looked up at Becky as if awaiting her response. Becky looked away.

"This circus has never hurt its animals," their mom said.

Jason rolled his eyes. "It's the principle that matters, Mom. Maybe there were slave owners who didn't whip their slaves, but that didn't make slavery okay. Did it?"

Becky's mom wagged her finger and nodded. "Your animal rights activism is really helping your critical thinking skills, Jason. But leave your sister alone."

Ten minutes before noon, the doorbell rang.

"Hi, Violet. Come on in," Jason said. "I know I can count on you to protest against the animal acts today. If I didn't have a football game, I'd go myself."

"No problem, Jason.

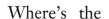

Where's the
T-shirt?" Violet asked.

Jason dashed upstairs.

"You're protesting at the circus?"
Becky asked Violet.

"No," Violet said. "But your
brother is something else."

"Tell me about it," Becky said.
"He's been bugging me all morning, showing me pictures of animals
chained up in filthy cages."

"How many teenage boys are so smart and
caring?" Violet asked.

"Huh?" Becky said.

Violet sighed. "Jason is so much more than
a pretty face."

"What?" Becky asked. "Are you going to
the circus or not?"

"Of course I'm going," Violet said. "I love
circuses. But I promised Jason we'd wear

animal rights T-shirts and we wouldn't ride the elephants at intermission."

"Bummer," Becky said.

Jason returned with two large T-shirts that pictured a circus trainer with a baton poised to strike a terrified elephant. "Aren't they great?" he asked.

"Unbelievable," Becky muttered.

The girls changed in the bathroom and zipped their sweatshirts overtop.

When they returned to the living room, they found Jason lecturing Scott and Nick and Mrs. Sherman. Jason held up a pamphlet showing whipped dogs and wounded lions. "I have some protest T-shirts if you want to wear them," he offered.

"Thank God you're ready, girls," Mrs. Sherman said.

"I have a video we could watch before you go," Jason said as they turned to leave. He

patted each of them on the back and added, "It won't take long."

"No, thank you!" Mrs. Sherman yelled as she hurried down the porch steps to her van.

Scott followed her. "What's on your back, Mom?" he asked. He peeled a sticker from his mother's coat. It showed an elephant weeping above the words *No animal acts!*

"There's one on each of us," Violet said. She peeled a sticker off Nick's jacket.

Becky climbed into the van and tried to disappear.

Jason waved at her from the kitchen window.

Why can't brothers just mind their own business? Becky thought.

#9: Boys will ask you out
and then ignore you.

Becky sat by the window in the very back of
the Shermans' van. Scott buckled up beside
her.

Mrs. Sherman pressed a button, and a television screen folded down behind her head.
Scott stared at it like he was hypnotized. Mrs.
Sherman nodded as if this was how things
should be.

As they drove away, Becky waved goodbye
to her mother, who was hanging garbage-bag

ghosts from the porch roof.

"Did you guys decorate your house for Halloween?" Becky asked Scott.

"Shush," he said. "I'm watching the movie." He didn't speak to her again until Mrs. Sherman parked at the stadium where the circus was playing. "Get going, Becky," he said.

They joined the long lineup in front of the building. "The afternoon show is always the busiest," Mrs. Sherman muttered. She looked around and scowled, like she was thinking all those other people should just go home.

"That's because they gave away so many free tickets," Becky said.

Mrs. Sherman cocked her head and squinted, as if Becky's words were hard to understand.

"We're still doing you a

favour by taking you," Scott said. "Even if Nick got your ticket for free, we still had to drive here and pay for Mom's ticket."

Becky wished she had come with her own mother. She tried to change the subject. "Look!" she said. "Those kids came in costume." A pair of vampires and a wizard waited in line ahead of them. "We should have worn ours."

"They're six years old!" Scott said.

Becky didn't try any more conversation starters.

Violet tapped her shoulder as they approached the doors. "See those protestors? I wonder if they know Jason."

"Who would want to stop a circus?" Mrs. Sherman muttered.

"Especially a free one," Becky said with a laugh.

Mrs. Sherman looked like she would have

shot lasers from her eyes if she'd known how.

"They want the circus to stop using animals," Violet said.

Becky launched into a graphic description of animal abuse in the entertainment industry. "They shock them, starve them, beat them on the head —"

"Enough!" Mrs. Sherman shouted.

Becky cleared her throat. "Not this particular circus," she added. "This one has never been charged with animal abuse. But they do have animal acts."

"So why did you come?" Scott asked her.

To be with you! she wanted to say — but Scott looked so angry that Becky just shrugged and muttered, "I thought it would be different."

Violet squeezed Becky's hand as they walked inside. "Don't be sad, Becky," she whispered. "Boys may be weird, but circuses are wonderful."

They found excellent seats facing the centre ring.

In the noisy hum before the show, Becky told Scott about the time she taught Champ how to dance like a circus dog. Scott nodded his head.

"He liked standing up on his hind legs," Becky said with a smile. "But he only did it to get his snout in line with the table and steal our food. Once he ate half a birthday cake before I could stop him."

Scott kept nodding his head. Becky noticed a wire sticking through his hair. She realized that he was nodding to his MP3 player.

She slumped in her seat. Beside her, Violet was cracking up over Nick's dog-ate-my-homework story. *I waited years to go somewhere with Scott Sherman*, Becky thought, *and it's the worst afternoon of my life.*

#10: Acrobats are awesome.

A man in a top hat addressed the audience in a booming voice. "For our first amazement, I give you the daring . . . the inimitable . . . Crazy Carlos!"

An acrobat bounced into the spotlight with a series of handsprings and cartwheels. He was the most beautiful man Becky had ever seen in her life, even counting the movies. He had wavy black hair, huge black eyelashes, sparkling blue eyes, and dimples in both his cheeks.

He was dressed like a prince in a loose silk shirt over black tights and slippers.

Becky dug her binoculars out of her bag.

Scott leaned over and asked, "Do you have any gum?"

"Shush," she said, waving him away. She gaped at Carlos for the next twelve minutes, entranced and barely breathing. When he performed his final triple somersault off a high wire swing, she jumped to her feet and clapped like a maniac.

"Sit down, for goodness' sake!" Mrs. Sherman hissed.

Becky barely noticed the next act, which featured clowns and jugglers and dancing dogs. But she sat up and screamed when Carlos returned to the ring. Three acrobats followed him, carrying a trampoline. "It's him!" Becky cried. "It's Crazy Carlos!"

"How can you tell them apart?" Scott asked.

Becky shot him a glance like he was insane.

The acrobats began to build a human tower. The first man backflipped off the trampoline onto the floor. The second man front flipped off the trampoline onto the first acrobat's shoulders. The third man somersaulted off the trampoline onto the second acrobat's shoulders. Carlos hopped onto the trampoline and began to bounce.

A drum roll sounded. Somehow Carlos had to fly across the floor and land on a pair of shoulders five metres in the air.

"It's too high," Becky groaned. "He's going to kill himself."

Crazy Carlos soared off the trampoline. He performed a flawless backwards somersault. He landed firmly on the shoulders of his brother acrobat. The audience cheered. Carlos stood proudly, one hand on his hip and the other raised in triumph, his white smile and blue eyes gleaming straight at Becky.

In fact, everyone in the circus was staring at Becky. That's because she was jumping up and down, rattling the chairs in front of her, and screaming at the top of her lungs, "He did it! Crazy Carlos! You did it! You're alive!"

Violet yanked her into her seat and clamped a hand over her mouth.

At intermission, Becky spotted Carlos at the elephant ride. "Let's wait in line," she said, dragging Scott by the wrist.

"You promised Jason not to ride the elephants!" Violet shouted.

Becky rolled her eyes. "If Jason were a girl and he'd seen Carlos, he would totally change his mind," she said.

"Is this your first circus?" Carlos asked when she and Scott reached the front of the line.

Becky — unable to speak or even swallow — nodded madly.

"I saw my first circus when I was eleven years old," Carlos said. "I went straight home to Florisburg and signed up for gymnastics. Maybe you will do the same."

"Sure," Becky said. "I dream about the high wire." It wasn't a complete lie — she really did have nightmares about heights.

Carlos smiled. "But first you want to ride an elephant, right?"

Becky's heart sank a little. She glanced at the sad old elephants walking in circles with squealing children on their backs. "No," she said. "I promised my brother I'd protest the animal acts while I'm here."

Carlos looked puzzled.

"Where is your protest?"

She pulled the crumpled elephant sticker out of her pocket.

Carlos leaned close so that Becky could have kissed him, if she wasn't frozen to the spot in absolute awe. "Next time, you should bring a bigger sign," he whispered.

He reached behind a concession booth and grabbed two sticks of pink cotton candy. "These are for you and your friend."

Becky turned to Scott with surprise. "Oh yeah. Hi, Scott. I forgot you were here."

"There you are!" Mrs. Sherman shouted from halfway across the ring. "Get out of that line right now! You can't go on an elephant ride!"

"Are you a protestor, too?" Carlos asked.

"No!" Mrs. Sherman snapped. "These rides are overpriced!" She grabbed Becky and Scott by the shirtsleeves and dragged them back to their seats.

"Isn't it wonderful?" Becky babbled. "Crazy Carlos is the greatest acrobat of all time."

Scott squirmed in the seat beside her. "What's so great about him?" he asked. "You're completely ignoring me."

"*I'm* ignoring *you*?" Becky said. "You didn't talk to me all afternoon. I don't even know why you asked me to come here."

"I asked you because I like you," Scott muttered. Then he put his earphones back in and turned on his MP3 player.

Becky shrugged. *I guess the only way to know if a boy likes you is to wait until he tells you*, she thought. *And even then, you can't be sure.*

Lesson 3: Geography

Tips for Surviving in the Middle of Nowhere

#11: Parents are allowed to drag you anywhere.

"Why do we have to go away on Christmas day?" Becky asked her parents for the hundredth time. She sat in the hallway, pulling on her winter boots. "Why can't Grandma come here instead?"

"Out the door," her mom said. "The school bus will be here in a minute."

It was the last day of school before Christmas vacation. Becky's class would perform a Christmas pageant for the school this morning. They would have a party in the afternoon, with homemade desserts and a gift exchange. It would be the best day of the year — if only Becky could stop imagining the holidays that would follow it.

She stuffed a tin of brownies in her school-bag. "Everyone else in the world goes south for the holiday," she muttered. "Why are we going to the North Pole?"

Her father stuck his head into the hallway. "It's not the North Pole," he said. "Don't exaggerate."

Her mother held out a pair of mittens. "We've been over this a hundred times, Becky. It's only five hours north. And it will mean the world to Grandma."

Becky pulled her

hat over her ears. "Why can't I have a normal grandmother who moves to Florida with all the other old people?"

Her father stepped into the hallway. He held a newspaper in one hand and a coffee mug in the other. "Stop arguing," he said. "You haven't seen Grandma since she moved up to Aunt Theresa's last spring. Think of *her* feelings."

"That's easy for you to say," Becky told him. "You're staying home."

Becky's dad raised the newspaper to cover his face, but not before Becky saw him smile. "I can't help it if I have to work," he said from behind the paper.

Becky's mom sighed. "Maybe I should go alone."

"No way!" Jason shouted from the upstairs bathroom, where he'd been eavesdropping. "I'm not staying home babysitting Becky while

Dad's at work!" He dashed to the top of the stairs with his toothbrush in hand. "She always complains before we visit Aunt Theresa. But she always has a good time."

"I do not!" Becky shouted up at him. "I make the best of it. That's a whole different thing from having a good time." She turned to her mother and father. "Of course Jason wants to go. He has Rick."

Becky's only cousin, Rick, was a sixteen-year-old video gamer who never said more than five words to her.

"People who live in the virtual world don't care if they're stuck in the middle of nowhere," Becky said. "But I care. There's no one for me to hang out with in the whole stupid town!"

"That's enough, Becky," her dad said sternly. "Your grandmother lives there now. You're spending the holidays with her. There's nothing more to be said about it."

"But why do we have to go for so long?" Becky asked.

"It's only ten days," her mom said.

"Ten days?" Becky shouted. "I can't go for ten days!"

Her father opened the door and nudged her outside. "Not another word, young lady!" he said. "You will go wherever we tell you!"

So much for freedom of speech and freedom of movement, Becky thought. *Families are not democracies.*

#12: If it's not a nice place to visit, be glad you don't live there.

"We're almost there," Becky's mom announced. "Thank goodness," she added. "It's black as night on this highway."

It was five o'clock on Christmas day. They had left home at noon after a long, happy brunch with Dad. "See you next year!" he'd shouted from the porch steps. "Champ and I will miss you! Wish we could be there!" Becky could have sworn she'd seen him dancing with the dog as they drove away.

Becky had been grumpy for the whole ride. She sat alone in the back seat beside a pile of books, crossword puzzles, and DS games. Jason was snoring in the front passenger seat.

Becky's mom slowed the car. The headlights shone on a sign that read, *Welcome to Florisburg, Population 3,500.*

"Why is that name familiar?" Becky asked.

"It's where Aunt Theresa lives," her mom said.

Becky shook her head. "No, that's not why. I heard someone talking about it."

Her mother shrugged. "It's not the sort of town that gets in the news."

Florisburg was almost buried in snow. As they drove in, Becky saw nothing but houses — no stores, no schools, no museums, and no movie theatres. The houses looked as if they just met there for the holidays, and would soon return to their proper towns.

"Unbelievable," Becky muttered.

Jason woke up and yawned. "I thought we'd never get here," he said.

They pulled into a long, circular driveway. Aunt Theresa's house twinkled with Christmas lights. A long ramp led to the front porch. A second ramp rose along the side wall to Becky's grandmother's apartment door.

Aunt Theresa stepped outside and waved.

Uncle Pete came out in his boots and coat. "Let me get your bags!" he said. He turned toward the house and called, "Give us a hand, Rick!"

Becky's cousin walked outside in his shirt-sleeves. He grabbed a suitcase from the trunk. "Hi, Jay," he grunted to Jason. "Hi, Aunt Margaret," he said to Becky's mother. Then he carried the suitcase to the house.

Becky gathered her books from the back seat. Everything was just as she remembered.

Jason and Rick would lock themselves in the basement and stink up the games room. Her mother and her aunt would drink tea and talk all day and night. Uncle Pete would work long hours out of town. And Becky would be left alone.

She grabbed her backpack and dragged herself into the house. It smelled like turkey and apple pie. A ball of mistletoe decorated the front hall.

Aunt Theresa kissed Becky's cheek. "It's great to see you, honey," she said. "I'm glad we could drag you away from your friends for ten days."

Becky imagined the fun she would miss over those ten days — playing hockey with

Stacey and meeting Scott at the pool. Even watching TV with Champ would be better than being stuck here.

"Head into the dining room," Uncle Pete told her. "We're almost ready to eat."

Becky shuffled down the hall. She bit her lip to keep from crying.

Grandma sat at the dining table in her wheelchair. She wore a shiny red dress with a silver necklace. She was all alone in the big room. When she saw Becky, she reached up for a hug.

"Oh, Grandma!" Becky shouted. She had almost forgotten that Grandma lived here now. She gave her a long, strong hug.

"My dear, sweet Becky," Grandma said. She buried her wrinkled face in Becky's hair. She clung to Becky like a lifesaver.

"Merry Christmas, Grandma," Becky said.

Grandma patted Becky's hand. "You sit here next to me, dear. I'm so glad you came. I have so much planned for us."

Becky kissed her grandmother's leathery cheek. "Is there a Bingo Palace around here somewhere?" she asked with a giggle.

"We might have to build one ourselves," Grandma answered with a smile.

Poor Grandma, Becky thought. *I might be stuck here for ten days, but she's stuck here forever.*

#13: Anywhere is heaven if there's an acrobat around.

"Let's bake cookies," Grandma said on Boxing Day morning. She pulled mixing bowls and wooden spoons from the cupboards.

Becky smiled. "Cookies are my favourite breakfast."

A dog barked outside. It reminded Becky of Champ. She glanced out the window. "Oh my gosh!" she screamed.

Crazy Carlos stood in the driveway of the house next door. A red toque covered his wavy black hair, and a red scarf covered his shiny white smile. But Becky would have known those blue eyes anywhere.

"That's where I heard of Florisburg!" she shouted. "It's Carlos's hometown!"

Carlos held a stack of presents in his arms. Two frisky poodles raced around his feet.

Becky jumped up and down. "We have to meet the neighbours!" she shouted.

"It's eight o'clock in the morning," Grandma said.

"We'll bring them some cookies!" Becky squealed.

Grandma smiled. "Good idea. They seem like a nice couple. Theresa introduced us when I first moved in. I think their son has been visiting for the holiday."

"Yes!" Becky shouted. "Their wonderful son is visiting! Look at all the presents he bought. And see how nice he is to the dogs?

He's a real animal lover." Becky sighed. "That's the acrobat I told you about, Grandma. That's the man I want to marry."

Her grandmother looked up in surprise. "He's thirty years old!" she said. "By the time you're ready to marry, he'll be middle-aged."

Becky waved away that idea. "Let's get a move on with these cookies," she said.

When the first batch was off the pan, Becky rushed next door with a paper plate stacked high. She skidded up the snowy ramp in front of the neighbours' house.

Carlos's mother answered the door. The dogs hovered by her legs. They barked and sniffed and tried to squeeze their heads outside.

"Hi!" Becky shouted. "I'm visiting my grandma next door. We made these cookies for you and your son." She tapped her toe on the threshold, hoping to be invited inside.

The woman glanced at Becky's boot with suspicion. "You must be Theresa's niece," she said.

"Yes! I'm Theresa's niece. I made these cookies for you and your son and any other acrobats who might be visiting."

"That's very nice of you." Carlos's mother took the plate of cookies with a smile. "You go straight home now. You'll catch your death of cold without a hat. Goodbye."

Becky raced back to Grandma's kitchen.

"We need something better than cookies!" she shouted. "We need a cake!"

Just then, Becky's mother knocked at the interior door that separated Grandma's apartment from Aunt Theresa's house. "Hi, sweetie," she said. "Violet is on the phone for you."

"Not now, Mom," Becky snapped. "We have a cake emergency."

Her mother scowled. "It's Violet's birthday," she said. "She's calling from Italy."

"Isn't it bedtime in Italy?" Becky asked.

"Becky!" her mother scolded.

Becky sighed impatiently and took the

phone. "Hi, Violet," she said. "Happy birthday. I can't talk right now because Crazy Carlos is visiting his parents next door and I have to bake him a cake."

"Carlos the acrobat?" Violet asked. "He's next door to you right now? In the middle of nowhere?"

"Yes!" Becky shouted. "Isn't that great?"

"You are *so* lucky," Violet said. "I won't keep you. We're going to the opera tonight for my birthday. We might have to come home a few days early. I'll call you tomorrow and let you know. Say hi to Jason for me. Bye!"

Becky passed the phone back to her mother.

"Carlos the acrobat is here?" her mom asked.

Becky nodded. "I'm making him a cake."

Her mother smiled. "I remember when I was your age," she said.

"So do I," Grandma said. She giggled and added, "I'll get the butter. You get the flour."

Becky washed the measuring cup. *An acrobat can really turn things around*, she thought. *There is nowhere else I'd rather be right now.*

#14: If you're living in a dream world, beware the wake-up call.

Becky rushed next door with a warm cake plate in her hands.

Carlos's mother frowned at her. The dogs squeezed their heads through the doorway. One dropped a squeaky toy at Becky's feet.

"Hello again," Becky said. "I made this chocolate cake for you and your son."

Carlos's mother sighed. "Come in," she said.

In the living room, an elderly man sat in a

wheelchair beside a sparkling Christmas tree. He waved and said, "I like cake."

Becky waved back. Then she asked, "Where's Carlos?"

"You must mean Ryan," Carlos's mother said. "I'll go get him." She disappeared down the hallway, shouting, "Ryan! A girl made you a cake!"

Becky was just thinking she'd made a terrible mistake, when Crazy Carlos walked into the hallway. He wore blue jeans with black socks and a white T-shirt. The dogs ran to him, wagging their tails as if they hadn't seen him for years. Becky felt like joining them.

Carlos stared at Becky with his handsome brow furrowed in concentration. Then he smiled and said, "Hello, protestor. Are you looking for elephants to save?"

Becky bounced on her toes, overjoyed that he remembered her. "Hello! I'm stuck here with my grandma, and we made you a cake," she said.

"Thank you," he said. He took the plate from her hands. "You're very kind."

Becky shrugged and blushed. "Why did your mom call you Ryan?" she asked.

"That's my name," Carlos said. "Crazy Carlos is just a stage name. I tried Reckless Ryan, but it didn't sound right."

Becky frowned. "Reckless Ryan sounds like a boy who falls off the jungle gym at school."

Carlos laughed. "And what's your name?" he asked.

"Becky Lennox."

"Did you move to Florisburg, Becky Lennox?"

She shook her head. "I asked my mom if we could go to Florida for Christmas, but she misheard."

Carlos smiled. "But really, aren't you a long way from home?"

"Actually, I'm visiting my grandma," Becky said. "She moved into my aunt's house next door. I don't think she likes it here. It's kind of the middle of nowhere."

"Tell me about it," Carlos's grandfather groaned from the living room. "Give me that cake, Ryan."

Becky wished everyone would stop calling him that.

The old man took the cake and wheeled himself down the hall. The dogs followed him.

"I can't believe you're here, Carlos," Becky said. "You're the best acrobat in the world."

He shook his head and smiled. "I think my wife is a better acrobat than me."

"Your what?" Becky squeaked.

"My wife," Carlos repeated.

"You have a wife?"

Carlos nodded. "She's upstairs packing."

"Because you're divorcing her?" Becky asked hopefully.

He looked confused. "No. We're visiting her family today." He checked his watch and added, "They live in Italy."

"Good cake!" Carlos's grandfather shouted from down the hall.

"You and your grandmother should come over tonight for coffee and cake," Carlos said.

"Really?" Becky asked excitedly.

Carlos nodded. "I'm sorry my wife and I won't be here. But I know my grandfather would like your company."

Becky's shoulders slumped.

Carlos picked a candy cane off the Christmas tree. He handed it to Becky. "A sweet treat for a sweet girl," he said. He smiled and opened the front door. "Please thank your grandmother for the cake."

Becky sighed. "Okay," she said. "Goodbye, Carlos."

"It's Ryan, actually. Goodbye, Becky. Have a happy New Year."

As she walked back to Grandma's apartment, Becky did not feel very happy. *I can't believe I gave away that delicious cake to some married guy named Ryan*, she thought.

#15: You never know what's around the corner.

It was New Year's Eve. Becky and Grandma had baked and chatted and watched television and played cards and sang Christmas carols all week long, until they were both bored senseless.

"I'll miss you when you go," Grandma said for the millionth time.

"You should get together with the old man next door," Becky said. "You have a lot in common. He doesn't like it here, either."

Grandma patted her wheelchair and sighed. "Maybe once the snow melts, I can make my way over."

"Get Uncle Pete to shovel a path between the ramps," Becky suggested.

Her mother burst into the apartment without even knocking. "Daddy's here!" she shouted. "And he has a surprise for you, Becky!"

Becky ran to the window. Her father's car was parked in the driveway. Champ ran around it, sniffing the ground. Becky's dad stood near the open trunk with two suitcases at his feet. When he slammed the trunk shut, Becky saw the most wonderful sight in the world: Violet!

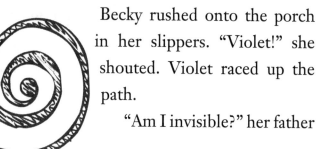

Becky rushed onto the porch in her slippers. "Violet!" she shouted. Violet raced up the path.

"Am I invisible?" her father

asked. "I rearranged my schedule and drove five hours to get here. This is the thanks I get?"

"Thanks, Dad!" Becky shouted. "Thanks for bringing Violet!"

Violet hugged Becky with all her strength. "My parents let me come!" she said. "Your dad said it was okay."

"Okay?" Becky repeated. "It's awesome!"

"I brought some fancy clothes for us," Violet said. "For tonight."

"What's tonight?" Becky asked.

Violet laughed. "It's New Year's Eve, silly. Don't you guys have a New Year's Eve party to go to?"

Aunt Theresa pulled the girls into the warm house. "There's a party at the dance hall every year," she said.

"Florisburg has a dance hall?" Becky exclaimed.

Aunt Theresa nodded. "Want to go?"

The whole family dressed up for the party. Jason and Rick peeled themselves off the basement couch and even took showers.

"Do you like my new dress, Jason?" Violet asked in the car.

He shrugged. "Sure."

At the dance hall, Jason and Rick sat in a corner watching a New Year's celebration on television until two teenage girls dragged them onto the dance floor.

"Too bad," Violet said. "I was hoping they would dance with us."

Becky looked at her like she was crazy.

They found a couple of boys their own age to talk to, but mostly they danced with each other and with Becky's mom and dad. Once, they wheeled Grandma around the dance floor with Carlos's grandfather.

It wasn't the best party Becky had ever been to, but it was the most fun she'd ever had in Florisburg. She wore a long pink dress and pink lip gloss, and she was allowed to stay up past midnight with her best friend. As the crowd counted down the final seconds of the year, she noticed an embroidered sign beside the dance hall clock. *Home is where the heart is*, it read.

I know just what that means, Becky thought.

Lesson 4: Mathematics

Tips for Solving 2 Minus 1

#16: Two is company, three is a crowd.

"I saw the first robin of spring today," Becky told Violet. They were walking home from school with their jackets slung over their arms.

"No way!" Violet said. "I saw a robin three weeks ago." She pointed across the street. "There's a robin on that lawn right now. And there's another one on the maple tree. And over there —"

"Okay!" Becky said. "I guess spring already sprung."

"You were too busy ogling Scott to notice," Violet said.

"I don't ogle Scott!" Becky said.

Violet laughed. "You've been in love with him since you started swimming lessons together."

"That's ridiculous," Becky said. Her swimming lessons had started in January. She'd been in love with Scott Sherman since kindergarten.

"At least you don't dump your friends for him," Violet said. "Have you noticed how Stacey acts since she fell in love with Josh Radcliff? She won't even sit with me if he's around."

"Josh is a nice guy," Becky said.

"But girls should never dump their friends for boys," Violet said. "I would never do that."

"Are you still coming

over to study?" Becky asked when they reached her house.

Violet smiled. "Of course."

They went upstairs. Becky dumped her schoolbag out on her bed. "Here's the textbook, but where are my notes?" she muttered. She looked around the room. "Violet? Where are you?"

"I'm in Jason's room!" Violet shouted.

Becky's brother sat at his desk in front of twelve plastic cups. Violet was leaning over his shoulder to see his notes.

"What are you doing?" Becky asked. "We're supposed to study in *my* room."

"Jason's working on a cool science project," Violet said. "He's making crystals. Grade nine is so exciting."

Becky snorted. "I made crystals in grade one."

"It's not just crystals," Jason said. "I'm

testing the properties of various fluids. See this?" He held up a cup of brown liquid.

"What are those white things in the bottom?" Violet asked.

"Teeth," Jason said.

"Teeth?" Violet repeated.

Jason had stolen all the baby teeth their mother had saved from when he and Becky were young. "Don't even say the word *tooth* around Mom, or she'll start screaming," Becky said.

Jason shrugged. "Keeping teeth is creepy. I'm putting them to good use." He smiled up at Violet. "They're dissolving in cola. They were much bigger two days ago."

"Amazing," Violet said. "What's in the other cups?"

Becky huffed into the hallway. "I'm going to my room. Come join me when you're ready to study."

After ten slow minutes reading her biology textbook, Becky stomped back to Jason's doorway. "Are you coming, or what?" she asked Violet.

"I have to run to the dollar store to buy some bristol board," Violet said.

"We don't need bristol board for a test," Becky said.

"I know. But Jason needs some to display his findings." Violet smiled and passed Becky a thick notebook. "I've already studied for the test. You can use my notes." She turned to Jason and asked, "What colour bristol board do you want?"

He shrugged. "Whatever."

Becky opened Violet's notebook. The pages were covered with detailed diagrams of amoebas, worms, frogs, and mice. Every anatomical term they'd ever used in class was defined in Violet's own words. "Unbelievable," Becky muttered.

Outside, Violet sprinted up the street toward the mall.

Becky couldn't believe that her best friend had dumped her for her brother's science project. *Talk is one thing*, she thought. *Life is another.*

#17: The power of one isn't all that great.

Becky and Scott walked to the skate park after their swimming lesson. "Are you sure Violet won't mind if I tag along?" Scott asked.

"She loves to teach beginners," Becky said.

The park was crowded with teenage boys. They sped down ramps, slid across railings, and jumped over stairs. They towered over the younger kids who were brave enough to join them.

Scott grimaced. "I don't think this is a

good day for my first lesson. I'll come back when it's not so crowded."

"You can't leave me until I find Violet," Becky told him.

Scott pointed across the park. Violet whizzed down one side of a concrete bowl and up the other. At the top, she jumped into the air and spun in a circle. "Can you do that?" Scott asked.

Becky shook her head. "I don't like the half-pipes," she said. "The low ramps are hard enough." She waved until she caught Violet's eye. Violet waved back. So did a teenager beside her.

Becky peered hard at them. "I think that's my brother, Jason."

She waited with Scott at the edge of the park for

another five minutes. "Did you and Violet have a fight?" Scott asked.

"No," Becky said.

"She's kind of ignoring you," Scott said.

Becky shrugged. "She's been acting strange since she turned twelve. Yesterday after dinner, she asked my mom if she could have a coffee."

"Coffee?" Scott repeated.

"Coffee," Becky said. "It's a weird phase."

"Like that weird phase you went through when you were in love with the circus acrobat?" Scott asked.

Becky scowled. "No! Not like that at all. That wasn't a phase."

Scott stared at his feet. "So, are you still in love with that guy?" he asked. "What was his name?"

"Carlos." Becky laughed. "But his real name is Ryan. I'm not in love with him. I can't

even remember what he looks like anymore."
She shook her head wistfully. "I should have
taken his picture — I don't know what I was
thinking."

"Maybe you'll see him again next year,"
Scott said, "if you come to the circus with me
again."

Becky smiled. "Okay. He was an awesome
acrobat."

Scott shook his head. "The acrobats on
horses were better."

"I don't remember them," Becky admitted.
She didn't remember a single bit of that circus
except for Carlos.

She dumped her bag of wet swim clothes
on a bench. "Do you want to sit down? Or we
could take turns on my skateboard?"

"Not today," Scott said. He sat beside her
with his bag on his lap. "Did I tell you I'm taking gymnastics?"

"Really?"

Scott nodded. "And this summer I'm going to a horseback riding camp. So maybe one day, I'll become an equestrian acrobat."

"Wow!" Becky said. "You want to be an equestrian acrobat?" Not only was Scott the cutest boy in her class, he was the most fascinating boy in the whole neighbourhood.

"Becky! Scott!" Violet shouted. She rode up beside them. "Where's Jason?"

"Who cares?" Becky said.

Scott pointed toward the street. "I think he left."

Becky's brother rolled down the middle of the road, crouching on his board.

Violet sucked in her breath. "I hope he doesn't get hit by a car. He's not paying attention to the traffic."

Becky rolled her eyes.

"I should go," Scott said. "I'll see you guys at school tomorrow."

"I have to go, too," Violet said. She rushed away without another word.

Becky was left alone on the bench next to her wet towel. She watched the crowd of kids having fun with their friends.

I turned down shopping with Mom and road hockey with Stacey so that I could meet Scott and Violet here this morning, she thought. *And look at me now.*

#18: Even mathematical geniuses are fools at heart.

Becky's class ran to their lockers before lunch recess.

"I'll grab a basketball from the gym," Scott told his friend Nick.

"I'll get one for us," Violet told Becky. "I'll meet you outside."

Becky searched her locker for a juice box. Nick hovered in the hallway, staring at her. "What?" she said.

He shrugged and said, "There's something

I want to ask you."

"Okay," Becky said.

Nick leaned in close and said, "Who is Violet going with?"

"Going where?"

"Going with," Nick repeated. "You know. Who's her boyfriend?"

Becky laughed. "She doesn't have a boyfriend. She's twelve."

Nick lowered his voice to a whisper. "I asked her to a movie, but she told me she's involved with someone else."

"Involved?" Becky repeated.

"Involved," Nick whispered.

"Wow," Becky said. "Involved is one step away from married."

Nick nodded. "So, who's the guy?"

Becky shrugged. "Maybe she made him up to let you down gently."

"I don't think so," Nick said. "She wasn't gentle."

"I don't know who it could be," Becky said.

On her way home from school, Becky dragged Violet into the playground on their street. "So, what's new, Violet?" she asked.

"Nothing," Violet said. She pouted on the see-saw. "This playground is for toddlers. Let's go to your house."

"I'm sick of my house," Becky said. "Jason's friends are always over. All they do is play video games and eat everything in the fridge."

"It would be better than staying here," Violet said.

Becky jumped off the see-saw. "Let's go by Stacey's house and ask if she wants to play ball."

"I don't feel like it," Violet said. "I think

I'll just go home." She wandered up the street and into her driveway.

Violet had forgotten her schoolbag under the see-saw. When Becky picked it up, a red binder fell onto the sand. It was covered in hearts and flowers with the letter *J* scrawled inside them.

Becky gasped. "Violet must be in love with Josh Radcliff!" No wonder Violet didn't want to go to Stacey's house — she couldn't stand the way Stacey ogled Josh. And no wonder she didn't tell Becky about him — she was afraid Becky would tell Stacey. It all made sense!

In science class on Thursday, Becky sat next to Josh. "I guess Violet must be home sick today," she said. "What do you think about that?"

Josh shrugged. "Maybe she has a spring cold."

"Did she say something to you about

having a cold?" Becky asked.

Josh scratched his head. "Why would she say anything to me?"

"I don't know. Maybe she tells you special stuff like that."

"Violet Turnbull?" Josh asked. He looked at Becky like she was crazy. "She never even talks to me."

Stacey squeezed in between them. "Are you guys talking about Violet?" she asked. "Did you hear that she started a pro-test to free the hamster in the kindergarten class? That girl is so weird lately." She made a face, then turned her back on Becky and made googly eyes at Josh.

When the bell rang at the end of the day, Becky gathered her homework from her locker. She grabbed a math book from Violet's locker, too, to go with an assignment she'd picked up for her.

She stared at a photograph inside Violet's locker. It showed Violet and Becky playing Frisbee in Becky's yard. Becky's brother, Jason, stood in the background, wearing an animal rights T-shirt and making a peace sign.

Suddenly everything clicked in Becky's head.

She knew why Violet had been acting so strangely. She knew why Violet dropped by Becky's house every single day. She knew why Violet was reading *Jason and the Argonauts*.

Because J is for Jason. *It could not be worse*, Becky thought. *My smartest friend has made the stupidest mistake.*

#19: Don't expect anyone else to learn from your mistakes. (Even you might not.)

"I invited Violet over tonight because her parents are working late," Becky's mom said. She frosted a cake at the kitchen counter. Fifteen spiral birthday candles lay beside the platter. "I hope you don't mind, Jason," she added.

Jason shrugged. "It's fine with me. It's not like my friends are coming tonight. It's just a family thing."

Becky's mom frowned. "Just a family thing?"

Jason smiled. "You know what I mean, Mom. It's the wonderful and joyous family dinner you made to honour my birthday."

"That's what I thought you meant," she said.

"I don't think you should have invited Violet to Jason's birthday," Becky said.

"I really don't care," Jason said.

"That's exactly why you shouldn't have invited her," Becky said.

"What do you mean?" her mom asked.

The doorbell rang. Becky checked the time: five o'clock sharp. She peeked out the front window. Violet stood on the welcome mat smoothing out her fancy blue dress. "You'll see what I mean," Becky said.

She opened the door. "Violet! Wow. You curled your hair."

Violet smiled and stepped inside. Her high-heeled shoe caught on the threshold.

She crashed to the floor.

"Are you okay?" Becky asked.

Violet frantically searched inside her gift bag. "Thank goodness I didn't crush the card!" she exclaimed. "It took me two hours to paint."

"Is that you, Violet?" Becky's mother said. "You're all dressed up, dear." She squinted and asked, "Do your parents let you wear makeup?"

"I'm not wearing makeup," Violet said. "This is just how I look." She batted smudgy black lashes and smiled a shiny pink smile. She reached into her gift bag and took out a cookie tin. "I made some hors d'oeuvres for the party, Mrs. Lennox. Where's Jason? I hope he likes his present."

Becky's mother stared at Violet in silence with her mouth hanging open.

"Now you see what I mean?" Becky said.

Violet picked at her dinner. She claimed to be on a diet. "A girl has to watch her figure," she said.

"A girl has to watch her sanity," Becky muttered.

Violet sang the happy birthday song like she was auditioning for a Broadway musical. "I sing and dance, as well as play piano," she announced.

"Unbelievable," Becky muttered.

Jason cut the birthday cake and passed out slices.

Violet said, "Just a tiny one for me, thanks."

"I could use a gigantic one," Becky said.

"Me, too," her mom agreed.

Jason opened his parents' present first: jeans, two T-shirts, and some cash to put toward his sports-car fund. "Sweet," he said. "Thanks, Mom. Thanks, Dad. I'll add this to what I earned shovelling driveways all winter."

Violet sighed. "You must be really strong."

Becky shoved her gift at Jason. He tore off the wrapping to find a book of card-game rules. "This is great, Becky. Thanks."

"Open my present now," Violet said. Her hand trembled as she held out a sparkling blue gift bag.

"You didn't have to bring a present, Violet," Jason said.

"I wanted to."

He pulled two video games from a pile of chocolate kisses. "Thanks a lot," he said.

"These are both top-rated games."

"I know," Violet said. "I looked them up on the Web." She sparkled and smiled and made googly eyes from across the table.

Becky grabbed another slice of cake.

After dinner, Jason took his presents upstairs to his room.

"Can we watch you play your new games?" Violet asked.

"No way," he said. "They're too violent for you little squirts."

"Happy birthday!" Violet shouted to his disappearing back.

That night after Violet went home, Becky crouched on the stairs and eavesdropped.

"You can't accept such expensive gifts from Violet," her mother said.

"I already opened them," Jason argued.

"Why is her scooter here?" her mom asked.

"She said I could borrow it," Jason said.

"Does Violet print your animal rights newsletters for you?"

"She asked if she could help."

"Do you not realize she has a crush on you?"

"Huh?" Jason said.

Becky's mother sighed. "Give her back her scooter, thank her for her help, and tell her very clearly that you are too old to be her friend."

"So I shouldn't let her do my book report for English class?" Jason asked. "All right, don't get mad!" he added quickly. "I'll tell her."

Becky shuddered on the stairs and remembered her crush on Crazy Carlos. *Poor Violet is headed for heartache*, she thought.

#20: Three years is a long time if you're twelve.

Becky and Violet were reading magazines on the porch when a fifteen-year-old goddess walked up the steps. She was tall and slender, with dark brown hair that cascaded around her pretty face and over her shoulders.

Jason rushed outside and kissed her on the lips. He put his arm around her waist and turned to Violet with a smile. "I don't know if you've met my girlfriend, Corinne, before," he said.

Becky and Violet were too dumbfounded to speak.

"Corinne," Jason said. "This is my sister, Becky, and her friend Violet. They are a couple of sweet little kids."

Violet ran from the porch in tears.

Jason watched her race down the street. He nodded and said, "That takes care of it nicely. Thanks, Corinne."

"No problem. I have to get back home now." Corinne smiled and added, "You owe me one."

Jason leaned on the porch railing, as happy as can be, and stared at Corinne as she walked away.

"You're a moron," Becky told him.

"What?"

"You are a moron," Becky repeated slowly. She walked down the porch steps shaking her head.

"What are you talking about?" Jason shouted after her.

Becky found Violet crying in her bedroom.

"I'll never get over him," Violet sobbed.

"Sure you will," Becky said. She stroked Violet's hair. "Focus on his worst points instead of his best points. Like Carlos being named Ryan — I don't feel the same about him since I learned that." Becky described Jason's most disgusting habits, all of which involved rude noises and foul smells.

Violet sniffled. "Thanks. I feel a little better." She looked up and frowned. "Why are you smiling? Are you happy that I'm sad?"

"Of course not," Becky said. "I'm happy that you're living in the real world again." She pulled a sheet of binder paper from her back pocket and held it out.

Violet unfolded the page. She read out loud, "*Thoughtless things Violet has done lately.*" She

looked up at Becky and asked, "Are you serious?"

Becky nodded.

"*Number one,*" Violet read. "*Stood me up at the skate park. Number two: came over and ignored me. Number three: spit cola at me to make Jason laugh.*" Violet shuddered. "I can't believe I did that." She continued reading. "*Number four: left me with all the work for our English report while she wrote some stupid thing for Jason's newsletter. Number five —*"

Becky grabbed the page out of Violet's hand. "That's enough," she said.

"I'm sorry I did those things," Violet said. "But I can't believe you kept a list!"

Becky laughed. "I couldn't help it. I needed proof that you're not perfect."

Violet sighed. "I'm nowhere near perfect. If I was perfect, Jason would like me."

Becky patted her back. "He does like you. He thinks you're awesome. He's just too old for you."

"I know. I wrote a poem about that for math class." Violet pulled a sheet of paper from her computer printer and read aloud:

Fifteen minus twelve is three.
Twenty-five percent of my life,
Twenty percent of his.
Too much, too much.
Put it in a circle and add up the angles.
Ninety degrees of my life,
Only seventy-two degrees of his.
Too much, too much.
Degrees of life, degrees of love.
Pi can measure circles
But it can't measure hearts.

"Oh, Violet," Becky said. "I hope you didn't actually hand that in for math class."

Violet swatted at her. They laughed.

"Want to go to the pool and hang out with Nick and Scott?" Becky asked. "They might not be as cute as Jason and Carlos, but at least they like us."

"Okay," Violet said. She blew her nose and wiped her eyes. "Thanks for being my friend, Becky."

Becky smiled proudly. She recalled her mother's favourite saying about love and friendship: If you love someone, set them free. *But if they fall for your fifteen-year-old brother, go catch them and drag them back to sanity*, thought Becky.

Lesson 5: English

Tips for Saying Sorry

#21: Honesty is not the most convenient policy.

Violet walked from desk to desk, passing out envelopes addressed in colourful calligraphy. "I'm having a pool party on Saturday to celebrate the end of grade six, and you're all invited."

The class buzzed with excitement.

Becky stared at the invitation. It read *Becky Lennox*, as if Violet needed to keep her straight among all her many friends named Becky. "When did you plan this?" she asked.

Violet shrugged. "A few days ago. I'm surprised Jason didn't tell you."

"What would my brother know about your party?"

"Attention, please," said Miss Nancy from the front of the room. "To celebrate the end of the year and all the hard work you've done, I've organized a class trip to Farley's Fun Park."

The students cheered.

Becky felt sick to her stomach. She overheard Nick telling Scott, "Farley's has the oldest roller coaster in the province. It creaks at every curve. It's just a matter of time before it speeds off the track."

Miss Nancy handed out permission forms. "The cost of the trip is eighty dollars. That includes your bus fare, entry fee, and ride bracelet. Anyone who doesn't want to go will join Miss Tanya's grade five class for the day."

Becky frowned as she skimmed the trip checklist: *sunscreen, hat, water bottle, lunch money, emergency waiver.* "What's an emergency waiver?"

"It's in case you die on a ride," Nick said.

A cold chill passed through Becky. "People die on the rides?"

"Oh no, hardly ever," said Violet from beside her.

Becky did not find these words comforting.

Stacey giggled. "The Whirlwind whipped me around so fast once I thought my head would pop off."

"I like the one that lifts you a hundred feet in the air and drops you straight to the ground," Josh said.

The paper in Becky's hand began to shake.

"What's your favourite ride?" Scott asked her.

"Becky doesn't go on rides," Violet said. "She's afr—"

Becky kicked Violet's leg under the desk. "Don't you have something to do for extra credit?"

Violet jumped to her feet. "I'll help Miss Nancy organize the trip!"

"Unbelievable," Becky muttered.

When the bell rang, the students rushed to their buses.

"Are you coming?" Violet asked Becky. "I have something important to tell you."

"No. I'll walk home," Becky said. She wanted to keep her feet on the ground.

Violet leaned against the locker beside her. "You're not going to like Farley's. You'll be too scared to go on the rides. And everything else is too expensive. You should stay here."

Becky looked her in the eye. "Would you stay with me?"

Violet stepped back in surprise. "No way! I'm not staying with the grade fives. I love amusement parks."

"You think I should stay with the grade fives all by myself? While you have fun with Scott and Nick and our entire class?"

Violet nodded.

"Not on your life," Becky said. "You better not tell anyone I'm afraid of heights."

This is the social event of the year, and I'm going to be part of it, she thought. *Even if it kills me.*

#22: If you can't say something nice, leave before you embarrass yourself.

"You're late for Violet's party!" Becky's mother shouted from the top of the basement stairs.

"So? She didn't even tell me about it until yesterday." Becky thumped up the stairs carrying a CD titled *Conquer your Fear in Five Minutes a Day*.

"Is that your father's hypnosis program?" her mom asked. Becky's dad had gotten stuck in an elevator for nine hours last year, and he hadn't been the same since.

Becky nodded. "I'll have to condense it a bit. Instead of five minutes for sixty days, I'll do sixty minutes for five days. Then I'll be ready for the roller coaster on Thursday."

Her mother patted her shoulder. "It's good you're trying, sweetheart. Now get to the party."

Becky's classmates were so busy swimming and playing volleyball at Violet's house that no one noticed her late arrival. Jason's friend Steve flipped burgers on an enormous steel barbecue while Jason threw beach balls and noodles into the pool and shouted, "No diving! No splashing!"

"What are you doing here?" Becky asked her brother.

"Violet's dad wanted someone responsible to work the party. He's paying me and Steve thirty dollars each to make sure you kids don't drown."

"Thirty dollars? Will you lend me some for my trip to Farley's?"

"No way," Jason said. "Violet says you're not even going on the trip." He turned to Josh, who walked by with a paper plate. "Meat is murder," Jason said. "Let me tell you how that's made."

"Becky, you're here at last!" Violet called from a lawn chair. She wore a pretty lavender dress over a wet one-piece bathing suit. "What took you so long? The band will be here any minute."

"A band is coming?" Becky said. "Why? Is it someone's birthday?"

Violet smiled. "No. It's just a party." She sat beside a picnic table crowded with chips and pretzels and a huge white layer cake that read *We Made It Through Another Year*.

"Where are your parents?" Becky asked.

Violet looked around and shrugged. "They don't micromanage." She smiled and asked, "Do you like my cover-up? Are you wearing a swimsuit under that?"

Becky raised her T-shirt a little to show off her bathing suit.

"You didn't get a new one for the party?" Violet asked.

Becky snorted. "Of course not. Did you buy new pyjamas for my sleepover last month?"

"Yes, actually. Didn't you?"

"Hi, Becky!" Stacey shouted. She walked over with three other girls, all wearing fashionable swimsuits and cover-ups. "Your brother tried to make us eat soy burgers. Let's see your swimsuit."

"It's her old one," Violet whispered.

Stacey frowned and muttered sympathies. "Violet told us that you can't come to Farley's on Thursday. That's too bad. We'll miss you."

Becky turned to Violet. "But you know I signed up for the trip."

"I didn't say you *couldn't* go. I said you *shouldn't* go," Violet explained. "You're scared of the rides, and you won't have enough allowance to play the games."

The circle of girls waited for Becky's response.

"I won't be scared of the rides," she said. "And my parents can give me money. Honestly. It's none of your business, Violet. Why would you tell people that?"

"You told me you're afraid of heights," Violet said.

"That was months ago!" Becky said. "And I told you in private."

"It's nothing to be ashamed of," Violet said. She looked around and announced, "Phobias are the most common mental illness in North America."

"I'm not mentally ill!" Becky shouted. "You're mentally ill if you think I'm suffering through Miss Tanya's class while everyone else goes to Farley's."

"That's nothing compared to what I'm about to suffer through," Violet said.

"You even have to be better at suffering than I am?" Becky whined. "You know, I have a lot to do today. I just dropped by to wish you luck with your party. Goodbye." She flung her towel over her shoulder and traipsed back across the street to her own house.

Sometimes a girl needs to make a dignified exit, she thought. *Before she says something mean and gets kicked out.*

#23: There's a good chance you're completely misreading people.

Becky was glad to have assignments to finish and fears to conquer all weekend so she could avoid Violet's texts and phone calls.

When she arrived at school on Monday, Violet's eyes looked red and puffy.

"Are you okay?" Becky asked. "Jason said your party was a big hit."

Violet shrugged. "It would have been nice if you'd been there."

Miss Nancy interrupted them. "Begin your

science presentation, girls."

"Why us?" Becky complained.

"Don't worry if you didn't finish your half," Violet said as she dragged her three-panel display to the front of the room.

"Of course I finished," Becky said, following with a bristol board. "I just don't want to go first."

"I thought you'd forgotten about it," Violet said. "You didn't answer my messages. So I wrote up both sides of the debate myself to make sure we don't lose any marks."

Violet's display was titled *Pros and Cons of Space Travel*. Beside it, Becky's display read *Pros of Space Travel*.

"Why didn't you just do your own work?" Becky whispered. "Now it looks like I only did half as much as you."

"You *did* only do half as much as me."

"But you weren't supposed to do my part!"

Becky snapped.

"Then you should have answered your messages!" Violet snapped back.

The week just got worse. Tuesday was track and field day. Only four girls participated in the 800-metre race. Stacey took the lead just ahead of Kaylee Hunter. Becky trailed a bit behind. Violet brought up the rear.

When Becky looked back, she saw that Violet had slowed to a walk. "I have a side stitch," Violet shouted. "You don't have to wait for me."

Becky shrugged. "I'll never catch up to

them. Besides, you look sad again today."

"I just don't feel like running," Violet said.

One hundred metres from the finish line, the gym teacher, Mr. Nesbitt, shouted, "Come on, girls! We need the track for the next race!"

Becky and Violet began to jog.

"Move it!" Mr. Nesbitt shouted.

The girls ran faster.

"Try your hardest or stay home!" Mr. Nesbitt shouted.

Becky broke into a sprint. Violet was right beside her. "Are you trying to pass me?" Becky panted.

"He said we have to try our hardest. What am I supposed to do?" Violet ran for all she was worth. She beat Becky to the finish line by two strides.

"This should really belong to you," she told Becky afterward, holding out the third place ribbon.

"No kidding," Becky said. "That was a dirty trick."

"But —"

Becky stomped home.

That evening, their mother sent Becky and Jason out to shop for their dad's birthday present. "It was just Father's Day," Becky whined. "How many ties can one man need?"

"Let's get him some weights," Jason said. His football coach had suggested a dumbbell routine for the summer.

"And some chocolate," Becky added. She had a sweet tooth.

In the mall, Becky spotted Violet and Stacey at the window of the pet shop, where two black puppies tumbled over heaps of shredded paper.

"She won't show up," Violet was saying. "She'll say she's not feeling well or something. She's way too afraid of heights to go. It would just be stupid. Nobody could be that stupid."

"Not even me?" Becky said, inches from Violet's ear.

Violet and Stacey screamed so loudly, they scared the puppies into a corner.

"You think I'm stupid?" Becky shouted.

"No! I didn't mean it like that," Violet said. "I would never say that about a friend."

"You're no friend of mine," Becky said. "You're a gossiping little know-it-all. I don't want to speak to you again."

She stomped down the mall, dragging Jason away from a pretty clerk in the chocolate shop. "Let's go," she said. "I have three hours of hypnosis to get through tonight."

I'll show Violet how wrong she is, she thought. *Then she'll be the stupid one.*

#24: Writing your life story requires a lot of editing.

On Wednesday night, Becky climbed up the spruce tree, branch by branch, repeating in her head, "There's nothing to fear. I am the master of my fate."

Champ lay at the bottom of the tree, watching her curiously.

She climbed seven metres upward before her legs refused to go farther.

She had a perfect view inside Jason's bedroom. He was lifting weights in front of the mirror with no shirt on. He counted out loud, smiling at his reflection. Becky wondered if Violet ever climbed this tree. "Are those Dad's dumbbells?" she shouted.

Her brother nearly jumped out of his shorts. "I'm testing them out," he said. "What are you doing in the tree?"

"Conquering my fear of heights."

"How's it going?"

"Pretty good." She straddled a branch and clung to two others with sweaty fists. "But I might need some help getting down."

Jason smiled. "Good luck at Farley's tomorrow."

"Is there anything to do there besides go on rides?" Becky asked.

Jason shook his head. "There are fairground games — you know, where you throw a dart at a balloon, that sort of thing. It's a total rip-off, though, like five bucks a game."

"Mom gave me fifteen dollars."

"That'll barely buy you lunch." He lifted a dumbbell over his head and lowered it behind his back. "Maybe Violet would give you some money. She's generous."

"I am not asking Violet for money! She doesn't even want me to go. She hates me."

Jason laughed. "You're crazy." He turned back to the mirror and did squats with the weights on his shoulders.

"Was she rude to you on Saturday?" Becky asked. "At the party, I mean. Did she boss you around or treat you like a servant?"

"Are you kidding? She kept offering me cake and thanking me for coming. She even helped us clean up. You could take some tips from her."

Becky sighed. In all the time she'd known Violet, she'd never heard her say a mean thing about anyone. "Do you think I overreacted?"

she asked, looking around.

From her perch in the tree, she had a perfect view of Violet's house. Mr. and Mrs. Turnbull were outside, showing off their landscaping to a man in a suit and tie. The man hauled a sign out of his car and hammered it into Violet's yard. A big white and blue wooden sign that read *For Sale.*

"Oh no!" Becky shouted. "Violet's moving away from me!" She looked at the ground. Her vision swam and her heart raced. Champ wagged his tail. "Jason?" Becky moaned. "Could you ask Dad to come up and get me?"

It took an extended ladder and Becky's entire family to coax her down the tree. When she finally stepped onto the ground, she smiled and squealed, "I did it!" Then she ran across the street to Violet's house. "Can I please speak to Violet?" she asked Mr. Turnbull.

"Becky? I'm surprised to see you. Violet told us you'd had a fight."

"Is she here? I need to talk to her."

"She's sleeping at Stacey's house tonight."

"Did she ask you to say that because she doesn't want to talk to me?"

"No!" he said in surprise. "She would never ask us to lie for her."

Becky sighed. "She's really at a sleepover on a school night?"

He smiled. "Don't worry. She took everything she needs for the trip tomorrow."

Becky had a sudden chill. "You're moving *tomorrow*?"

"No, no," Mr. Turnbull said. "I meant the trip to the amusement park. But you won't be going on that, will you?"

"Oh yes I will," Becky said.

She marched home and put the hypnosis CD into her player.

Some friendships are so important, they're worth conquering your worst fears for, she thought.

#25: Always try for a happy ending.

Becky made a beeline for the tallest, most terrifying roller coaster in Farley's Fun Park. Nick and Scott joined her in the lineup, followed by Violet.

"You can't go on this ride, Becky," Violet said. "You'll have a heart attack."

"So you keep telling everyone," Becky muttered.

"Why would you come to an amusement park if you're afraid of heights?" Nick asked.

Becky shrugged. "People do silly things because they want to be with their friends."

Violet stiffened. "Like throw an enormous pool party for the friend who goes home in a huff?"

"You didn't throw that party for me!" Becky exclaimed.

"Yes, I did," Violet said. "I thought you'd chicken out of this trip. I begged my parents to let me have a party so you could celebrate with the class."

"That can't be true," Becky said.

"How would you know?" Violet asked. "You left. I had to sit through that lousy band all by myself."

"You weren't by yourself. You were with Stacey," Becky whined.

"I wanted to be with you, too."

"You told everyone I was afraid of heights!"

Violet shrugged. "You *are* afraid of heights."

Becky shook her head. "I did a hypnosis CD to conquer my fear."

"Those things work?" Scott asked.

Becky looked up at the roller coaster as the cars screamed past. "I'll soon find out."

"It takes years of therapy to cure a phobia," Violet argued.

"We don't have years," Becky said. "Why didn't you tell me you were moving?"

Violet stared sadly at her feet. "I just found out. My dad got a job offer in California a couple of weeks ago, but he didn't decide to take it until Saturday. I didn't want to let it ruin my party."

Becky tried to imagine poor Violet getting the news. "I guess I ruined it instead," she said.

Violet sighed. "Yeah. You did. But Jason was a big comfort."

"Jason? My brother?"

"I watched him swim for half an hour.

That cheered me up." Violet giggled and added, "Do you think he Skypes?"

Becky rolled her eyes.

"My parents bought me a new laptop with an awesome webcam," Violet said.

"Maybe I could learn to Skype so we can keep in touch," Becky said.

Violet looked her up and down. "I thought I was a gossiping little know-it-all."

"I thought I was stupid and mentally ill," Becky said.

Violet smiled. "I didn't mean to hurt your feelings." She shuffled ahead with the moving line. "But this ride...Never mind. I don't want to be a know-it-all."

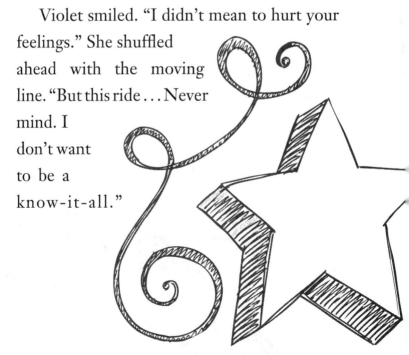

"You're not, Violet. Not really. You're a great friend. I'm so sad that you're moving. I'll miss you so much."

Violet squeezed Becky's hand. "Me, too."

Nick shrugged. "California sounds pretty good to me."

"I want this to be your best day ever," Becky told Violet. "I'll go on all the rides with you. It's my way of saying sorry."

Violet grimaced. "You won't die in my arms or throw up on me, will you?"

"Of course not." Becky looked at the lineup, which had grown surprisingly short during this conversation. "At least I hope not," she muttered.

"Don't worry," Scott said. "It goes so fast, you won't have time to be scared. You won't throw up until it's over."

Becky followed Violet up a metal stairway and along the track to the very last seat of the roller coaster. "Are you sure about this?" Violet asked. "A note of apology would have been enough."

"I'm sure," Becky said, fighting the panic rising inside her.

The safety bar lowered and locked in place over her chest and hips.

"Oh my gosh," Becky muttered.

Violet grinned. "You're stuck here now."

The cars began to crawl slowly up the track. Becky watched the ground move farther away. "It's not actually that bad," she said optimistically.

The first car passed over the crest of the track and led the train of passengers plummeting to the ground, then up the next loop.

"AAHHHH!"

Violet laughed and screamed.

Becky cried and screamed.

If I survive this ride, I'm smashing that CD into a thousand pieces, she thought. *From now on, I'm going to listen to my best friend.*

Becky's Last Tip

#26: If you have a sense of humour, an annoying family, and an open heart, you already have everything you need to survive.